Ruby and Leonard

and the

Great Big Surprise

Judith Rossell

LITTLE HARE
www.littleharebooks.com

This book belongs to:

_____

Little Hare Books
8/21 Mary Street, Surry Hills
NSW 2010 AUSTRALIA

www.littleharebooks.com

First published in 2009

National Library of Australia
Cataloguing-in-Publication entry

Rossell, Judith.

Ruby and Leonard and the great big surprise / Judith Rossell.

9781921272967 (hbk.)

For pre-school age.

Mice--Juvenile fiction.

A823.4

Designed by Vida Kelly
Produced in Singapore by Pica Digital
Printed in China through Phoenix Offset

54321

Ruby and Leonard lived behind the
biscuit tin at the back of the cupboard

with all their brothers and sisters.

One day,
Leonard
had an idea.

He whispered his plan to Ruby.
'But it's a surprise,' he said.

'So we can't tell the others?' asked Ruby.
'That's right,' said Leonard.

'Now, all we have to do is follow the instructions.'

'It will be easy,' Leonard said.

First, they
measured
the sugar.

And weighed
the butter.

'This is almost
easy,' said Ruby.

'Beat until fluffy,'
shouted Leonard.

'Okay, I think that's fluffy enough!'

'That was a bit less easy,' said Ruby.

They measured some vanilla essence. 'Hold the spoon steady,' said Leonard.

Next, they broke some eggs.

'Eggs are easy to break,' said Ruby.

'The others will be so surprised,' said Leonard.

'Secrets are fun!'
agreed Ruby.

They sifted the flour
and measured the milk.

'Stop coughing, Ruby,' said Leonard.
'You'll give away the surprise.'

'I'm not coughing,'
said Ruby.

They mixed everything together in a big bowl.

'Pay attention, Ruby,' said Leonard. 'We're nearly finished.'

'We just have to bake
them in the oven.'

'Did you hear whispering?'
asked Ruby.

'I thought it was you,'
said Leonard.

'Let's rest, while they bake,' said Ruby.

They waited and waited.   And waited.

Until at last the cakes were baked.
'We did it, Ruby!' said Leonard.

'Now for the icing ...
but stop squeaking,
Ruby, or the others
will hear you.'

'Just a drop of colouring ...

but stop giggling,
Ruby, you'll give
away the secret.'

'I can't wait to show them,'
said Leonard.

'Can you, Ruby?'

'Ruby?'

Leonard called again.
But there was no answer.

'Ruby?'

'Anyone?'

'Surprise!'

'Happy Birthday, Leonard!'

'Happy Birthday, Ruby!'

'Happy Birthday, EVERYONE!'

Cupcake Recipe

Cupcake Ingredients
1 cup castor sugar
100 grams/ 3.5 ounces butter
1 teaspoon vanilla essence
2 eggs
2 cups self-raising flour
1 cup milk

Icing Ingredients
2 cups icing sugar
2 tablespoons butter
2 tablespoons water
Food colouring
Sprinkles and little sweets
An adult to help

Preheat oven to 200°C/ 392°F. Beat sugar and butter together until fluffy.
Add vanilla essence and eggs and beat well. Mix in sifted flour and milk. Add more milk
if the mixture is too dry. Line cupcake pans with paper cases, fill each case three-quarters
full and bake for about 15 minutes or until golden in colour. Cool on cake rack.

To make icing, beat together icing sugar, butter and water. Add a few drops of food
colouring. When the cupcakes are completely cool, spread the icing with a knife.
Decorate with coloured sprinkles or little sweets.

Makes about 24 cupcakes.